RELIVE

RELIVE

Margarita Evangelista

Library of Congress Control Number: 2018907240
ISBN: Hardcover   978-1-9845-3614-3
                 Softcover   978-1-9845-3613-6
                 eBook   978-1-9845-3612-9

Print information available on the last page.

Rev. date: 06/19/2018

To order additional copies of this book, contact:
Xlibris
1-888-795-4274
www.Xlibris.com
Orders@Xlibris.com
780322

There are a lot of things that you cannot see, hear, taste, or touch. You cannot see feelings, but they can certainly touch your life. They are the best glue to remember the best of your life. Every moment that sticks with you is glued by the touch of your feelings, and they are permanently stamped in your heart. We can overcome events in our life, and I learned that when you feel weak is when you become stronger. You never know how strong you can be until you have to be strong.

Day by the day indeed goes as when you are sitting outside on the porch, just looking at the cars passing by fast. Sometimes it is hard to count them or even distinguish one color from another just as they pass in front of you. And as you wake up every day to go to work, if you do not hold on to matters of importance, then any other person not much different from you in other parts of the world did so too. They wake up and take the same way to go to work, and life can turn monotonous. As you see the sun coming up for everyone and every day, we can also see it dawning as if it were born every time. Because as the baby cries, the sun gives the bright rays.

Time might pass, but the lessons that it gives stay, and on no account will they go away and will surely never get old or monotonous. Growing is a part of life; life goes on, and you collect good and bad experiences along the way, but both help you become who you are and find your journey. Believe me, nothing is in vain not because you need to pass from all of it but because you turned them into good. Nevertheless, you always have the power to shine like the faithful sun. You cannot forget the sun because it is there and always remind you of the goodness of God. Memories, as the word explains itself, cannot forget because they always remind you of the goodness. Time will pass, and with it, people will come and go, be born and die. But never forget that the greatest glue of all stays with you forever; that will never die, and that will never get old or fade away. Memories always bring moral of a fable. Just turn around and look at the right angle, and you may see the right prospect.

I remember as if it were yesterday. These moments are still vivid in my mind, and my heart still beats to it that, even today, I get to revive them. I do not know if you would understand me expressing that I found myself crying inside out. It is as if you would or could disgorge your guts, and as powerlessness come to pass, you will not be sure if you are feeling numb, feeling dead for a second, or just feeling as if you were walking in a rope in a high landscape then falling and not knowing when you will actually hit the bottom.

Like any other day of the week, in that morning, the alarm rang at six o'clock. I got up, got ready to go to work, and then woke Jacob up. He was my five-year-old son. I was a teacher in the same school that he was going to. Just like a regular day, he went to his classroom, and I went to mine. Nothing much was different from any other day.

We went home after school. On our way home, we always talked about our day. Jacob always liked to share ideas from what he learned. I always thought that he was really smart. I would say anyone could enjoy his company. Jacob told me that he had to sing for his first play, but he was too nervous and shy about it.

When we got home, we did his homework together, played a little after it, and started to cook dinner. Jacob liked to bring out the ingredients and help out with dinner. Kevin usually got home at three o'clock, but on Fridays, he would get until five thirty in the afternoon, which meant that he had Saturdays off for family activities. As soon he opened the door, Jacob knew it was Dad. Just like regular parents, to spend more time with our kids, we let Jacob sleep a little late than the other nights. Jacob was telling Kevin how nervous he was about the play and that he did not want to do it.

Kevin told him, "Today I woke up earlier than usual because, by eight o'clock, I was supposed to be at the court for a case. The judge is there and the audience too. Guess what, I do get nervous about it, but I do it, and its feels much better after you do it. And as they want to hear me, probably, a lot people would like to hear you too."

Saturday morning, Kevin and I woke up and shared about our work. We were getting ready while waiting for Jacob to wake up since we had planned to go to the beach for a picnic. But he received a call from his business partners. Both were lawyers, but Kevin kept some papers that Brian, his business partner, needed. We agreed that he could go and drop it, and we would wait for him. It was ten o'clock in the morning when Jacob woke up; he got ready and had some breakfast.

He noticed that Kevin was not there, so I told him, "Daddy had to go and drop off some paperwork, and he will come back to go to beach."

It took him a little longer. It was noon, and he called me he was just getting back home. Thirty minutes after, I spoke to Kevin. It started to drizzle, and then a few seconds after, it turned into a thunderstorm. Unbelievable that nature could transmit the coming disaster by sight; it could touch your senses and heart that it would shake all your being. Hail was falling, and it felt, from time to time, that the roof would crash and break by the trembling. It was hard to see because of the wind. There was a lot of traffic affected by the rain; it looked as if someone were pouring water at your window. Plus, the wind made it worse as if it were possible that the thunder was mad, looking to damage and aim at the target. It was gray—the type of gray that looked as if the sky were suffering by it—and you could feel it just by looking at your body. Easily, the image was stamped, and goose bumps were the result of what was coming. By the clouds, you could really clearly see the coming event, even though you could hardly see outside. Anything that you would see through a mirror looked distorted. You could not tell if the object was close or still far away from you.

Kevin was still on his way back home. The wind sounded like a whistle. You could see the trees bending. You could hear the thunder as if it were next to you. You could see the lightning and feel the trembling on the floor. Kevin was only about ten minutes from home.

I was with Jacob in the living room, waiting for Daddy; we were having hot chocolate with marshmallows and cookies.

Kevin was stuck on traffic because it was only a two-lane road. He was coming from the city, and he just saw a shadow in his right side that moved so fast and then disappeared from his sight. He got a car ahead of him. Everyone was driving under the speed limit. On the left side of the road, the cars were going to the city, and there was a big truck of heavy load. The shadow that Kevin saw was a motorcycle. The driver of the motorcycle was not able to control, and it was hard for him to see. Kevin was mostly scared because he could not see what was really going on around him. He got in the way of the truck. The truck tried to brake, but there was a lot of water on the pavement that caused the truck to hydroplane. The truck slipped into the right lane. Silence and suspense were printed in the seconds that were passing and flying. The truck collapsed on its side. There was a collision in the middle of the uncertainty. Then police and paramedics came to the scene.

Certainly, the driver of the motorcycle was dead. The car that was ahead of Kevin received a great impact, and the driver was unconscious and in a critical state. Kevin also was unconscious and in a critical state since the tension was more than painful. And you could feel the seconds more than the actual beats, and in each spin, your heart would spin as well. He was not able to see much, but it was more than enough to hear the sounds. Kevin had fainted with all the commotion that he was involved. He was pushed away by the car. The truck just flipped around in circles, spinning faster, causing him shock, and then he fainted. Most of the vehicles' tires couldn't grab on the road because there were a lot of hail and water, and it was hard to maneuver anything at the time. It was hard to believe that he was close, just ten minutes away from home, at the same time still far away from me that I could not even imagine the nightmare.

While waiting for Kevin at home, Jacob and I were in the living room when I received a call from the hospital. I ran to the phone to answer it. It was a nurse telling me that Kevin just got into a serious car accident, that he was unconscious and in intensive care. I took the phone and moved to the kitchen to avoid Jacob hearing the conversation. I told him, "I'll be right back," while he stayed, playing and watching TV. In one second, it felt as if someone threw a bucket of cold water over my head, leaving me cold as my heart beat faster.

It felt as if my stomach shrank with all my emotions in it. My body and mind were empty as if I were in space but, at the same time, were thinking all these thoughts and feelings messing me up like a tornado, razing with my insides. I hope he was okay. Adrenaline was all over my body because of all these emotions in me, and then my body got warm.

I had a lump in my throat, choking on the feelings. It hurt in the intended swallowing. I had the urge to see him and hold him into my arms.

Meanwhile, the nurse was still talking. I asked her the address of the hospital where he was taken in, and I wrote it down. But the nurse told me that I probably could not go to the hospital because the main road was closed and other roads were also closed for safety reasons. I felt that the agony just got longer. I asked the nurse if I could at least speak to the doctor who was in charge.

She said, "He might call you back," and I said okay and then hung up the phone. I called my parents; they lived twenty minutes away from home. I explained the slightest information that I knew. Therefore, they were determined to come home and stay with Jacob or, if it was necessary, to take Jacob with them to their home. After talking to my mom, I stay seated on the kitchen table for a couple of minutes, trying to think what I was supposed to tell Jacob. It felt as if the time just got prorogated, and at the same time, you could hear the seconds. I went back to the living room, and every step that it took to get there, I was thinking what I should say. I sat next to him and told him, "I do not think we can make it to the beach today."

He replied, "Yeah, I guess because it is raining. Right, Mammy?"

His answer tasted like a bitter bite I had to swallow because the next thing I had to explain was that Daddy was not coming home. I took a deep breath—one of the heaviest ones that I had ever had to take—and told him, "Daddy is not coming today because of the thunderstorm. He had a little trouble coming, but you might see him soon."

I was hoping that Jacob did not have so many questions because each word was ripping me into pieces. Jacob asked me, "Can I see him tomorrow?"

"I do not know, but I will let you know when you can see Daddy. But guess who is coming today? Grandpa and Grandma."

Jacob got excited about the idea of them coming to our home; they would come after the storm subsided. I had the phone close to me, waiting for the doctor's call. I just had a call from Brian. It was three forty-five when the storm started to settle down. Meanwhile, I was trying to do my best to play and be a great company for Jacob. We went to the kitchen because Jacob was a little hungry, so I cooked macaroni and cheese and chicken nuggets. I washed the dishes while Jacob ate. The doorbell rang; I went to see who it was. I opened the door, and it was my parents.

When I saw them, I just wanted to hug them just like when I was a child and just feel comforted by them. But I did not want to cry, so I just said hi.

I told my mom and dad, "Thanks for coming." I offered them something to eat or drink, but they read my mind.

My dad said, "Go if you have something to do, and we'll stay here with Jacob. Do not worry we can talk later."

My mom hugged me, and she told me, "I love you, honey."

I told her, "I love you too. Jacob is in the kitchen, eating. I probably have to make some calls, and I am thinking to go to the hospital."

I called the hospital, asking for Kevin. The nurse told me that he was stable, but he was still sleeping. "Sorry that Dr. Lee has not contacted you yet. We are really busy, but I ensure you that we are taking a great care of your husband."

I told her, "Thank you. I probably would get there soon."

The nurse told me, "Okay then. Take care and see you."

Then I called Brian. I told him everything about the accident and Kevin's condition. Brian told me not to worry about anything right now. "Just be with him and take care of him, and I promise I will take care of the law firm."

Brian and Kevin were not just business partners of the law firm. They knew each other from elementary school. Even though they grew up in the same neighborhood, they became best friends in middle school. Kevin was an only child, and Brian only had a younger sister. Both went to the same university; they became brothers and best friends. They got dreams and goals together. Brian met Emma in high school when she became part of the group and also Brian's girlfriend.

I moved to their neighborhood when Kevin was in university. Even though I was not going to the same university as him, I saw him every day because I was his next-door neighbor. Also, I saw them hang out a few times at Kevin's house when I was coming back from university. After two weeks, Kevin finally decided to say hi to me and welcome me to the neighborhood.

He said, "Hello, I am Kevin. He is Brian, and she is Emma. Welcome to the neighborhood."

I told him, "Thank you. Great to meet you. I am Gabrielle."

We all shook hands, and Brian said hi, and so did Emma. Kevin and Brian graduated from the university as lawyers. Emma who got married to Brian graduated as a pediatrician. On the other hand, I graduated as an elementary teacher. Emma and I became best friends as well. Without planning, we got pregnant almost at the same time. I was pregnant of Jacob when she also got pregnant of Rose. Emma was Jacob's pediatrician, which made it a lot easier because Emma was family and a great friend to Jacob too.

I thanked Brian for taking care of the law firm and told him he was such a great blessing and support in this crisis and just like an elder brother to me. His automatic reflex was always to protect Kevin and me since I was an only child in my family too.

I told him I was going to the hospital. Brian told me that he will try to go to the hospital the next day. I told him, "Thank you again, and see you tomorrow. Say hi to Emma and Rose."

I called a taxi because I thought that I could not drive since I had a lot in my mind. I changed my clothes and told my parents, "I am going to the hospital, and any other news that I might have, I will call you. I love you, Mom and Dad."

Jacob was in the tub, playing with bubbles. So I told Jacob, "Bye, honey. I have to leave and see Daddy, but Grandpa and Granny are staying. I love you, Jacob."

I kissed him on his forehead. The taxi was already outside of the door. I asked the driver to take me to the hospital and gave him the address. I got all mixed feelings again, probably because I had not been able to talk too much to avoid crying. I was excited just as when he went to visit me when we were dating. I felt anxious to hear Dr. Lee telling me Kevin was great. I also felt sad and concerned how I was going to react the next time I see him. I was trying to look for encouragement. My heart was beating hard that I felt its echo everywhere.

It was almost five o'clock when I got to the hospital. I went to the receptionist who was in front of the main entrance.

"Hello, my name is Gabrielle McGates, and I am looking for my husband Kevin McGates. He is in intensive care."

He said, "Room 210."

I answered him, "Thank you."

I got to the room where Kevin was. Good thing that a nurse was still there. "Hello, good evening. I am Mrs. McGates. Do you think that I can talk to Dr. Lee?"

She replied, "Let me look for him." Then she left the room. As soon I saw Kevin lying on the bed, I felt relief, in peace, just thanking God that he was alive, just with some bruises. However, I was still concerned why he still had the oxygen and why he was still asleep. I just stopped wandering around, and then I approached him, kissed him in his forehead, and whispered, "I love you a lot, and I miss you with all my heart."

As I was looking at him, I remember how he proposed to me. "Remember when you proposed to me? You invited me to ride our bikes and go to the park. I told you why you want to go now because it was late. It was 6:30 p.m. You told me that because you never ride your bike with the sunset and you wanted to do it for the first time with me. I said, 'Okay. Let me go and get my bike.' When we were almost there, you went ahead and pretended that you fell down from your bike. Then you acted as if you got an injury and as if you were in pain. You told me that you thought that you sprained your ankle.

"Then I got down from my bike and went right away toward you. I hunkered down to help you, and all of a sudden, you were on your knee, asking me, 'Can you cure me forever and give me the honor of marrying me?' I always like your uniqueness in doing things. They always have a touch. When I saw the ring, I wanted to cry of excitement, not because of the shine of the ring but the one in your eyes.

"The ring was not just a symbol of the time you put into picking it but of the feeling that you have toward that special someone you are proposing to. When a man gives a woman a ring, he is not just giving her a diamond, but his heart is with it. I answered you, 'Yes, I would be honored to be your wife and hold your heart and take care of it.' That day, you gave yourself to me, and I am still keeping you with me."

I kissed him on his lips and told him I would be right back. I went to the hallway and asked a nurse that I was looking for Dr. Lee.

She said, "Come with me."

She took me to his office, and she went to look for him. After a couple of minutes, Dr. Lee came to the room.

He said, "I apologize for all the delay. I'm just being more busy than usual."

I answered him, "It is okay. I would like to know more about my husband Kevin McGates' state."

"Kevin is okay. Besides some bruises, he got two ribs that were injured, but nothing to be alarmed with. He is still in intensive care because I am just waiting for him to wake up. His breathing is better than before, so we are thinking of taking the oxygen off. He is a lucky man, considering the accident that he was through. To tell you the truth, I have not had the chance of watching the news. Well, the man from the motorcycle is dead as well as the man who was driving in front of Kevin.

"Kevin received quite an impact, but he just got some fractures, and he does not have any major damage. We are just waiting for him to wake up. Most of the patients do not wake up right way because it is a part of the recovering. We had made some scans, X-rays, and all that is necessary to ensure you that we have checked organs, brain, and bones. When he wakes up, he can go home."

I told him I was thankful for the care that they were giving to him. I went back to his room.

I called my mom to tell her that I was going to stay in the hospital with Kevin, that I wanted to talk to Jacob but I was just waiting for Kevin to wake up for me to talk about Daddy. The doctor told me that there was not a need for me to stay in the hospital in case I wanted to go rest. Since Kevin was not awake yet, there was nothing much I could do—just wait. He told me that was my decision; that if I wanted to, I could stay too. I stayed with him because I wanted to be there in case he woke up.

I lay down next to him, in that small space. I closed my eyes and took his hand and held it. I heard a mumble close to me. As soon I heard it, I opened my eyes and got up. There was Kevin, finally awake from his sleep. I did not know what to do. I was happy that I saw him awake but concerned that he could not move and he just mumbled. He looked at me with eyes wide open, and I worried that he did not know what was going on.

I came close to him, and while looking directly into his eyes, I told him, "Thank God you are awake! Stay calm and do not worry about anything now. The important thing is that you are back to me again. I love you, and let's just be happy for this . . . I will get the doctor."

I went out of the room, terrified by what just happened inside. I did not want to show it to him, but my heart broke into pieces just feeling impotent and useless, of not being able to do anything but just talk to him.

I went out looking for Dr. Lee. After I found him, I told him that Kevin just woke up but he was just able to mumble and he could not move at all. He was also as concerned as I was. He said aloud that that was strange. He went with me to see him. He checked him again and then told us that all the results were in a normal level, that Kevin did not have anything abnormal or a great injury that could cause this damage. He said that if we would redo the test, he was sure that it would yield the same results.

I was sitting next to Kevin while the doctor was in front of us. He said that he had a case just like this before, that his brain was in an auto-defense mode, turning off all the system because of shock from the accident; that Kevin probably reached a high level of adrenaline, causing his brain to erase some information; and this meant that he had to relearn things like when he was a kid.

"In medical terms, he did not sustain any injury that fizzled out his brain and body capacity, but psychologically, it is a mechanism of defense to protect him from serious damage. He recognized people and things. Generally, he does not have posttraumatic amnesia due to a head injury. Traumatic amnesia is often transient but may either be permanent or temporary.

"The extent of the period covered by the amnesia is related to the degree of injury and may give an indication of the prognosis for recovery of other functions. Mild trauma, such as a car accident that results in no more than mild whiplash, might cause the occupant of a car to have no memory of the moments just before the accident due to a brief interruption in the short long-term memory transfer mechanism. The sufferer may also lose knowledge of who people are, and having longer periods of amnesia or consciousness after an injury may be an indication that recovery from remaining concussion symptoms will take much longer.

"The other one is transient global amnesia. It is a well-described medical and clinical phenomenon. This form of amnesia is distinct in that abnormalities in the hippocampus can sometimes be visualized using a special form of magnetic resonance imaging of the brain known as diffusion. Symptoms typically last for less than a day, and there is often no clear precipitating factor or any other neurological deficits. The cause of this syndrome is not clear. The hypothesis of the syndrome includes transient reduced blood flow, possible seizure, or an atypical type of migraine. Patients are typically amnesic of events more than a few minutes in the past, though immediate recall is usually preserved. But between these two categories, because even though that he did not forget the information about people, his brain forgot the memories about the physical ability because he mumbles, which means he wants to talk."

Dr. Lee also added that the hospital got services, that if I wanted to have a nurse and physical therapist at home and some help around the house, they can provide too. He told me that it was healthy and better for Kevin to have a family environment instead of being at the hospital, and since he did not have any medical need to be in the hospital, it was better for him to stay at home.

"I am going to keep evaluating him during the night and tomorrow morning. And if Kevin is doing great, does not have anxiety or panics attacks due to circumstances, he can go on Monday."

I was happy with the idea of him being at home, around all the people who actually loved him and care for him. It was just perfect for Kevin so he could go back to normal again.

After talking to the doctor, I decided to call my mom and to tell her what was going on with Kevin's health. She told me even though it sounded hard, least there was hope for him, and that she knew that I was brave and strong to go through it.

I replied, "Thank you, Mom. I love you very much too. I should probably try to make time to go and talk to Jacob about Kevin. See you soon, and I love you. Say hi and thanks to Daddy and that I also love him too. Bye."

Then I hung up, and I took a deep breath and smiled and told Kevin, "My mom and dad say hi, and they both cannot wait to see you soon. Jacob is with them."

And right after I mentioned Jacob, his eyes got bright, and he smiled. I smiled again after him, but this time, there was happiness in it. "You are going to see him soon, and he probably is going to be glad to see you too." I had a lot of thoughts in my mind, but I was smiling and telling him that we were going to be fine, that he was going to be the same after everything passed through.

"Brian and Emma say hi, and Brian says that do not worry about the lawyer firm, that he will take care of it, and that they both love you deeply. Let me lie next to you," I told him, "and hug you tight. I love you, honey.

"Remember when I used to hug you just like this in your backyard and look at the stars? Well, let me look at your eyes. Can you see the glow in my eyes? I am very happy to be with you and to know that this is just temporary." Even though I was always trying to be cheerful, my heart was broken in pieces, full of impotence, and always wondering what was in his mind.

I told him, "Let me go for a little to the hallway to call Emma, okay? I love you."

It was funny, and I was curious that when I went outside, I noticed more things because when I came a few hours ago, everything was just blocked out my sight, even the sounds. I guess I was desperate to see Kevin. The nurses were coming and going. I could hear monitors, and I also saw families looking after another member of their family. All these people together in the same place were trying to see a hope or were just happy to see one, including me. But something was for sure—you could hear more the beat of the hearts of the people than the monitors or any other noise. Your heart bled out of anguish, but instead, your face reflected hope.

I called Emma to update Kevin's state. She answered the phone right away. I told her that Kevin was stable but that he might have some physical therapy because, even though his memories were intact, his capacity of moving—such as walking, chewing, or moving any other muscle—probably will have to be stimulating again, just like a little kid.

"He also mumbles. That means that he will easily talk again, but it will take a little bit of time to develop it again. I am glad and excited but just worried. How am I supposed to explain it to Jacob?"

She told me, "Do not worry. You will know when the times comes, you will see."

"Well, thank you and see you soon. Say hi to Brian and Rose. Bye."

Before I went back to Kevin's room, I took a look once again around my surroundings, and I just thought, Thank you, God, because he is alive and full of hope.

I opened the door, and I smiled at him, and I felt in peace knowing that we were strong for the things that were coming. It was 7:30 p.m., and since he was awake for a few hours, we would probably not sleep soon. I was trying to figure out how to communicate better with him.

Then I remembered a case back in the university while I was studying psychology, a little girl could not talk caused by the violence done to her; so every time someone asked her something, if the answer was yes, she blinked once, and if the answer was a no, then she blinked twice.

I told him that. And if he was comfortable enough to do that, at least until the doctor removed the cast of his neck, then he could nod.

The expressions in his eyes were overwhelming as he was just trying to digest what was happening to him and all of us. There was no complain or reproach. However, there was concern.

"Can we try?" I asked him. He blinked his eyes once, and he did it slowly, and he tried to grin a little.

"Are you hungry?" I asked him. He blinked once, so I called the nurse and asked her if they could bring some food for Kevin.

She answered back, "Yes. Just let me see the diet for him, and I will get something for him.

I told her, "Thank you."

While we were waiting, I decided to just ask him questions to find out how he was feeling.

"Would you like to go home tomorrow?" He blinked once.

"Do you know that you might need a physical therapist, and a nurse probably will stay with us, right?" He blinked once again.

"You might need a wheelchair to move around the house until you are able to walk again." And he blinked once for the third time. Then a nurse came by, bringing some food for Kevin. It was oatmeal, orange juice, and a paste soup that was easy to swallow.

Before he ate, the nurse, while taking the cast away, added, "It was just to protect him when the paramedic took him from the accident in case of any fracture, but Dr. Lee will check his neck again to make sure if he still need it. For now, you can eat without it," and she leaned the bed in an angle that was safe and comfortable to eat.

Then she said, "Let me show how to feed him. This angle is easy for him to open enough to make it safe to swallow. You will put the spoon almost halfway, take out slowly the spoon, and he will swallow a lot easier. Since he is able to open his mouth, anything that is smashed, such as liquid or soft paste, he is going to be able to swallow. Would you like to try it?"

I replied, "Yes, I would like to."

So the nurse waited to see how I was going to do it to make sure I was doing it the right way. Then she said, "I see that you are doing well, so I'm just going to give you time, and I will go. Anything that you need, just give a call or just press this button right here in the left side of his bed. My name is Patricia, and I am the designated nurse for him, and I am going to be the nurse who is going to be at your home to help around. Pleased to meet you, Mr. and Mrs. McGates. If you'll excuse me."

I told her, "Pleased to meet you too."

After I finished feeding Kevin, Dr. Lee came by the room to see how we were doing. He said, "Hello, how are we doing so far?"

I told him that Kevin just finished eating, and I fed him. Dr. Lee said, "Maybe the nurse told a little about his diet, and obviously, she taught you how to feed him also. His diet is pretty much any vegetables, fruits. If he eats chicken, it has to be really liquid until we are sure that he swallows really well to make it like paste, just like baby food's texture.

"The nurse who is taking care of Kevin has been the same nurse since he came to the hospital. She knows a lot of his case, and she is a specialist in this matter, so she will know what to do. Let me check your neck."

He straightened the bed. He moved Kevin's neck from left to right, and then he softly let go little by little to see how much Kevin was able to hold. Kevin was able to hold his head; therefore, he told us, he might be able to use a wheelchair or sit without any problem. He was sitting straight, and his body was not heavy for him since he could stay without falling to the sides or falling right in front. He checked the rest of his body, such as arms, legs, fingers, feet, and hands. All these extremities of the body were not able to move. He asked Kevin if he could try to move his neck sideways. Kevin did it in a slow motion, not all the way, but he was able to do it enough to see that his neck was perfect; it just needed more exercise to develop more muscle again.

"Well, I see that Kevin is doing great, so if you would like, you can leave tomorrow, and Patricia will go with you, and she will keep me updated until the next checkup for Kevin.

"The physical therapist will go every day. Until he sees a difference, the visiting will reduce to fewer days per week. He also is also going to give a report every week or as needed. His name is Matt, and you are probably going to meet him before you go home. Here is my information in any case you needed it, and the nurse has it as well.

"If you'll excuse me, see you tomorrow right before you go home, if you decided to go tomorrow. In case that you have to prepare anything before Kevin and you go back home, you can go until Monday, okay? Well, take a good care of both."

I guess we would have to decide as things flow along with time. I would dare to say that being in the hospital just made things harder because anyone could become more vulnerable; in my personal experience, I would say that it felt as if I were limited to actually have a normal conversation or reaction to such a situation.

As me, I could sometimes hear the silence as well as I could see people suffering. It was true that it was not a place like home. I was yearning to be at home with the surrounding that Kevin and I needed to survive to all these feelings and events. There was one more thing I had in my mind—the urge to see Jacob and talk to him and somehow prepare him on the things that were coming along with the changes and explanations of all questions. I just want to enfold in Kevin's arms and cry and tell him I was okay and he was going to be great, but every time I would see his eyes, I had the steadfastness that I needed to not convey anything to him but strength.

Just being in the room felt suffocating, so I called a nurse so she could help me put Kevin in a wheelchair, and we could go around the hallways, just to not go crazy in the room. Every time I came back there, it felt even smaller. The nurse told me that she probably would have to ask the doctor's opinion, but she would come to the room as soon as she gets to speak with Dr. Lee. I approached Kevin and told him that I wanted to just go around the hallways so we could have fresh air.

Then the nurse came into the room and told me that it was okay, and she helped me transfer Kevin into the wheelchair. She added that Dr. Lee thought that it was not bad idea since he did not have any fracture or big damage, but we still have to be careful. After the nurse helped me, Kevin and I went for a walk until we got into a waiting room.

The waiting room was surprisingly beautiful. I would say, coming from a hospital, perhaps I was waiting for something depressive. On the left-side corner was a piano next to it. In each side were six long couches making a rectangle, and in the middle a table. In the right side was a wall; at the center of the wall was a flat TV, right in between the piano and the five tables for people to eat.

I took Kevin, and we headed to the piano. I placed him next to the piano, and I sat on the couch next to him. I felt peaceful. We were just starting a new journey together.

"Even though this is just the beginning, I know within me that soon we are just going to remember this," I told him.

Then I sat down at the piano and asked Kevin if he remembered the song "River Flows in You" that I used to play when we were going out.

"Would you like me to play it?" I asked him.

He nodded very slowly, so I played for him. I knew it by heart, so the whole time that I was playing, I was looking and smiling at him. It is mysterious how a part of you can become forgotten with the time passing by and how ironic life can be when you get reminded by the circumstances that you go through. I used to love playing piano. It was like having a diary anytime that if something happened, I would play, just as writing on the pages made you feel better.

Right after I finished playing the piano, a nurse passed by the waiting room. She was amazed by the melody and said, "I like it. You play really good."

"It is refreshing knowing that. Thank you," I replied to her. I asked her, "Please do not mind me ask. Why does the hospital have a beautiful room like this one?"

"Do not worry," she said. "A lot of people asked that same question as well, but we have long-term patients who also need some cheering, so the hospital created this for them and their families for a little bit of joy."

It's almost unbelievable how a room could bring you joy, and I felt alive one more time. Afterward, I sat again next to Kevin. I kissed him on his right cheek and said, "You are my best melody. Let's go back to the room so you can rest."

We got to the room, and I called the nurse back for aid to put back Kevin into the bed. It was late, and Kevin looked tired, so I just told him, "Good night," and gave him a kiss on his forehead. I lay down on the bed that was next to his bed. I could not sleep because all this that was going on my mind and thrilling in my body made me feel poignant. I did not feel sad but a soothing comfort.

I woke up, and I looked at the time. I guess I went to sleep a couple of hours. I slowly went to see Kevin, and he was still asleep.

He looked as peaceful as when a baby is really tired; he just conveyed tranquility. Well, it was just five thirty in the morning. I went to look at my cell phone, and I saw a text message from Brian letting me know that he was coming to the hospital between eight and nine in the morning. Hence, there was a lot to do. I decided just to go home and rearrange anything that had to be done before Kevin's return. Furthermore, I probably needed to talk to Jacob. I went out of the room, looking for a nurse at the same time I was calling a taxi; then I saw her, and I told her to tell Kevin, in case he woke up before I come back, that I just needed to go home but would come back as soon as I could. Subsequently, I went out of the hospital and waited for the taxi to come; probably, I just waited five minutes in which I took advantage and called home to let my parents know that I was heading home.

The whole way home, I was just thinking how awkward or how much difficult it would be to have to talk since I left home; it just felt as if I were gone for weeks. When I got there, everything looked different to me; there was an empty feeling as if I were a stranger. I was not talking about the way it looked but the way I felt; I got to see things in a different perspective. Most likely, I knew it was my home. However, I was just pursuing not happiness anymore but just something simple—a routine filled up things that I could not remember when I started liking them and, at the same time, things that I just forgot in time. As I just stared at the corner where I could see nothing but an empty couch and a table with an orchid, I just could place a piano to play with Jacob and have fun with it. Being in the hospital changed me too. From the storm that I thought broke my heart and ruined our life, I actually saw a new meaning of life. Just a little bit far to the right, I saw a rainbow—a wonderful hope.

I would not dare say that I had figured out everything by now, but at least I did not have sorrow or any complaint with life. Even though my heart was still beating, it was hard to see what reaction I would have from Jacob. The suspense was thrilling. In the intervening time, I had to clean the guest room and fix it up for Patricia. Afterward, I went to Jacob's room that was at the other side, and my parents were with Jacob, sleeping in his bed.

I smiled; it just reminded me when I was a little girl. I closed the door again very carefully; I went down stairs to my room to prepare everything for Kevin's arrival. Right after I was done, I decided to go to the store to get grocery and get ready when they come home. When I came back, I decided to cook breakfast and prepare some fresh orange juice. I was not sure if it was the smell of the food or any noise that I did, but my parents and Jacob woke up almost when I was just finishing to put the dishes away.

Jacob shouted, "Mommy!"

I felt so happy that I could express my gaze. Then the suspense was gone almost immediately, and it was just peace and a release of feeling of gladness. We sat at the island table that was in kitchen. Almost as soon as we started eating, my mother asked, "So how is everything?"

I looked up and said, "Everything is going to get much better, I can ensure you that."

"Where is my daddy, Mommy?" Jacob asked me.

I told him, "Honey, unfortunately, Daddy had an accident, and that it is why when he comes back from the hospital, he is not going to be the same. But that is just going to be for a term, and Daddy is going to need our help to the same one again."

"What does he have, Mommy?" Jacob added.

"Well, he had a big shock, just like when you go to a roller coaster or if you got a big surprise. So it was a lot for him to take. Now our job is to help him and show him that we love him a lot and he will get better. Daddy is coming today, and like a baby, he will not be able to talk or walk, so we might have to help him."

Jacob replied, "Okay, Mommy. I want to help. I love Daddy, and we can show him that we love him just as he and you taught me when I was a baby, right?

"Yes, honey. When you have any questions, come to me, and I would help you. I might have to go get Daddy and bring him back home, and we will have a guest with us. She is going to be Daddy's nurse. Her name is Patricia, and you will meet her soon. I love you. Can you give a kiss to Mommy? So I will be back soon."

I went outside and got the truck, and before it turned one, I decided to call Emma and ask her if they were going to the hospital.

Emma told me yes, they were about to leave, and I asked her if they could come to the house instead and wait for me and Kevin at home. Then she told me that Brian probably would like to go, but she and Rose could go home and wait with my parents and Jacob. I also thought that was a great idea, so I agreed to it.

"Thank you," I told her. "I do appreciate your support. See you soon." Then I drove to the hospital and went straight into Kevin's room. He was awake, and the nurse was there with him when Brian got there. He knocked on the door since he knew that the nurse was there; he opened the door and then saw him.

"Excuse me," Brian said. "Hi, Kevin. Forgive me for the excitement." And Brian could not hold the gladness that was for him to see Kevin again and hugged him. Afterward, the nurse left the room. Brian looked at Kevin with grateful gladness. "I am thankful today because you are here alive. The day I knew about the accident, I was scared of the idea of losing my brother, but now I just thank God. You are with us, and the rest is just piece of cake, and we can all get through this together.

"Do you remember all the things that we passed through when we were young? We took an oath with a salt pact, meaning that we were supposed to eat food that was preserved in salt. And in my culture, we are just allowed to eat with family and close friends, not with any guests because it means that when we eat salty food together, we are doing the pact of being brothers that only death can separate us. It means loyalty of brothers. And since that we are just as the best brothers, thanks for fighting for your family. It is good to reminisce. We are in this together. You got my shoulders, never forget."

Brian, just like me, would want to read or know what he was thinking to know better what to do or say. Brian added even though Kevin could move his neck and he did facial expressions, I guess, at that time, it was hard to read what Kevin wanted to transmit.

I arrived at the hospital thirty minutes after Brian got there. I passed trough the hallway, almost straight to Kevin's room. I went in the room, and I saw Brian. We both said hi at the same time and hugged each other, not as a consolation but more as an agreement that we were together in this, and we felt encouraged once again.

I approached Kevin and told him, "It is time to go home. Jacob knows about you, but he knows that you had an accident but not in detail. He is okay with the news, and he wants to be there for you too. Brian wanted to take you home, but actually, I just got informed that it's necessary for your safety to go in the ambulance. And Brian is going with you in the ambulance, and he is okay to pick up his car in his way back home. On the other hand, Patricia is going with me so we can talk more about your case and talk as well about a few things about her staying in the house.

"I love you, Kevin. I could say I know you know it. But I love you with all my heart. In my mind, this is just an opportunity to show you my heart even more, for you to see in my eyes that I'm not petty. But every time, no matter what, I fall in love with you all over again. Right now, I just want to tell you that I felt my heart squeezed and my life froze a little, but now, when I see you, I feel the deepest, purest love and gladness of you being with me. I love you forever and ever. I will see you at home. I'm just going to sign the discharge and get Patricia. She is probably in the waiting room. I love you more than ever because I know that you woke up for us and you are fighting for you and for all of us as well. And that shows me your love and strength."

Then I kissed him on the forehead and told him, "See you in our home, my love," with a huge smile, hoping a bright sunshine of bountiful blessings waiting for us. There were two paramedics who went with Kevin and Brian in the ambulance. All the way home, they were quiet. But certainly, there was a connection because there was a part as if they both knew what they were thinking, smiling just as the same time when Brian took Kevin's hand. And for the first time, Brian prayed in his mind. Kevin knew he was praying because Brian closed his eyes. Brian was loyal, and his custom was so faithful and strong in each meaning. They did not pray because they did not believe in God, but he was raised with determination and discipline and, moreover, loyalty of what he was.

On the other hand, Kevin came from a Christian family. He would pray, and they both respected their differences. And even though they did not say anything, they both learned from their background and culture. They both went through a lot, counting that Kevin was the only child and that his mom was a single mom and that there was a time when Kevin did not have more family than his mom and Brian.

Patricia and I were on our way home, and she was explaining to me the probability that Kevin had; that she had seen so many cases; that his case was one among many; that when it was caused by a trauma, people get too traumatized that it was hard or almost impossible to recover; but she was sure that everything would turn out good. I was listening, but inside of me, I knew that this was just transitory, not because she was telling me but because I just knew it in my heart.

When we got home, the ambulance and everyone else were awaiting. I told the paramedics to come inside the house, and we went inside, and everyone else were in the living room, waiting for us. Then Jacob saw Kevin coming through the living room.

Jacob shouted, "Daddy! I love you, and you will see how we are going to be closer than ever."

Then when Kevin was settled in the room, my parents and Jacob came by to the room. Jacob sat next to him, and my parents were standing while the paramedics were placing all the equipment and supplies. Patricia was helping them.

My parents told Kevin that he got their support and that he would always be their son and that he got their strengths. At first, I did not get what that meant until later on. Then they left. Patricia stayed in the room while I went to say bye to my parents and the paramedics as well.

I told my parents, "Thank you for your support."

They replied, "You are welcome. You will see how you and Kevin will overcome this event."

Then I showed Patricia her room and around the house, while Brian and Jacob were in the room with Kevin. After I showed Patricia her room, I went back to my room, and Emma, Rose, Brian, and Jacob were there.

Brian told him, "See you later."

Emma told him, "Bye, Kevin. I utterly know that soon you will be telling this just as a story."

Rose told him, "Bye, Uncle Kevin. You know I love you, right? So do not forget I will come and visit you, and you will see how much fun we are going to have."

So they left. Patricia came by, asking if I needed anything. I answered, "No, thanks," and she said she would be in her room for a little just to review information. I sat on the coach chair that we had in the room while Jacob was next to him.

Jacob told Kevin, "Daddy, I am glad you are home despite whatever. My longing is just to show my love. And do not worry, I am always going to be by your side."

I was pretending to read a book while listening to him. I knew that he was a smart kid, but I was not expecting that because, actually, every time that he approached Kevin, every step of the way, he always had the perfect words to heal our hearts with comfort and sureness. I went to Patricia's room just to tell her that I was about to put down Jacob to bed and that we have monitors with cameras in most of the rooms that were needed to have a better control of Kevin. Then I went with Jacob to his room, put his pajamas, and helped him brush his teeth. When I was putting him into bed, he told me, "Mom, I love you."

I gave him a kiss and told him good night. I went out of his room, and it is curious how one could still hear the ticktock of the clocks in the midst of silence. I was just trying to keep myself together from time to time so I would not fall apart. How could you tell your heart the thing that it wanted to hear when there were no words?

I got to our room. I sat next to him and held his hand, and I told Kevin, "Remember when Jacob was born that day, you told that God is always good and the living proof was Jacob and the beautiful life. Indeed, God is truly good. I am blessed by your life, and I am glad for holding your hand."

I prayed that night, and to tell the truth, I could not remember when was the last time I prayed, but I certainly felt alive once again. When I opened my eyes, I just saw his eyes were open, and he got the spark that you could see when you know that you were not alone, that you have hope, and when you find yourself once again because you feel the strength you thought was not there anymore. For sure, there were no words, and there was silence after that, but it was accompanied with a big smile and full of strength. We just saw each other in the eyes, and there was no explanation but a simple assurance that everything would be all right. I told him, "Good night, my love." I just kept on smiling, and he grinned at me.

I would never have the right words for or explain enough the irony of how not having words connects us in a different way. Just by telling myself and remembering that, I got the chills and goose bumps like electricity running all throughout my body, an overwhelming feeling that someone is experimenting how bright you can feel, expressed through your eyes and skin.

That night, I could not fall sleep, not because of worry but because sometimes time froze and memories ran. As certain as blood running through the veins, they also ran, shaking every particle of your body, and the rest did not matter anymore now when you clearly see your way.

The next morning, Jacob had to go back to school, and I stayed with Kevin that day. All the clouds dissipated. I decided to stay at home and help Kevin with his recovery as I was also planning to homeschool Jacob kindergarten, teaching both of them at the same time. At the time, I was not sure if it this would be a good idea, but I got the feeling it would be a good experience for Kevin and for Jacob as well. That morning, we started the physical therapy in all his body—arms, legs, back—for him to start handling the weight. I knew it would be intensive because there were a lot of things to be done for him to start having the sense of touch again and, moreover, the mobility for everything. There were exercises even for the hands, wrists, ankles, and so many more.

In the afternoon, I went to pick up Jacob and talk to the principal of the school to present my resignation letter, explain my decision, and tell her that I was thinking that, eventually, I would like to teach Jacob at home; that it was just a matter of some rearrangements. She understood the situation and told me that the doors of the school would be always open for me since I was one of the best teachers, academically speaking.

"Thank you," I said, and then I went for Jacob in his classroom, and then Jacob and I went home.

During the drive, I was explaining to Jacob that I was not going to work anymore at the school because I wanted to stay with Daddy and help him recover his talking skills. And eventually, if he liked the idea of studying together with Daddy, it would be great; but if he wanted to stay at school, it would be okay as well. What I wanted was that Kevin had his son as a company of learning, and I knew deep in my heart that it would be not only a great bonding but also a great encouragement for Kevin and joy for Jacob to share with his daddy.

But I would still leave up to him. I also told him that for those following weeks, he would start to ride the bus until we could decide what he wanted to do. When we got home, Jacob wanted to go see Kevin before homework time. We went to my room. He was in the bed. Jacob sat next to him and started talking to him, telling him about his day.

"Daddy, Daddy, I had a great day at school today. There was a fire fighter, and he showed us what to do in case of an emergency. Look at these stickers." Then he went to play at the backyard. I went to the kitchen and cooked some dinner for everyone.

We all ate at the dinner table, including Patricia, since I thought this type of environment was healthier for Kevin. Kevin was sitting on a wheelchair, and Patricia was feeding Kevin, while I was finishing serving the food and putting it on the table. We used to talk a lot during dinnertime, and after I was done eating and Jacob too, Patricia sat on the other chair since she knew how to feed Kevin. Even though Kevin knew how to move his jaw, it was just for safety since she got the experience. Even though Kevin did not have trouble swallowing at this point, it was a regulation of the doctor's orders.

Well, I sat next to Kevin, and Jacob sat on my lap. I read to them Jacob's favorite books that he used to read at nighttime. Somehow we did through with the organization of all the things and schedules. While I was putting the plates in the dishwasher, Jacob was telling Kevin how to say some words. He used to tell him, "Daddy, repeat after me, Daddy. Say, 'I love you.'"

Right after I heard that, I turned around. Kevin was trying to mimic the sound. I was shocked because I could see the effort that he was doing to at least mimic the sound of those words. Patricia and I smiled; it really was as if the clouds were starting to dispel.

"Mommy! Mommy! Daddy tried to say 'I love you.' Did you hear that? Did you hear that, Mommy?"

"Yes, I actually did, sweetheart. Thank you for helping Daddy." He burbled the word, but it was just as if I got to breathe again after drowning and had the relief of seeing the light again. My body felt a matchless hope. Everything in life is transient, but we have to endure to be able to conquer.

Despite everything, my best interest was always to transmit to Kevin a warming, normal, and loving environment and never do anything that could make him feel he was a burden. That night, after I tuck Jacob into the bed, Patricia and I put Kevin in the bed. She went to her room, and I started talking to Kevin while massaging his arms and hands and doing some exercises and movements to help his muscles and nerves. I talked and smiled. Time flew that night as the stars froze through the window, giving light, infusing our vivacious connection of appreciation and love for each other etched by that night.

If anyone would tell you their life story, none of them would actually have expected certain events in their lives.

Who would say that there were moments that you might not appreciate as much as when you had to pass through them; how, in a blink of an eye, your life would dramatically change? In just 180 degrees, everything turned around, and then it's just as if you were dreaming alive, feeling impotent and numb, trying to wake up, but you could not because it's not a dream. But absolutely, in the way things settled, you started to breathe once again.

Well, I was starting to breathe again. Every second that I spend with Kevin was just a gift. And to know that I could finally see myself in him once again, in some way, I came back home again because I found myself. As I said before, I would look back once again and find my heart through Kevin's accident because instead of losing myself into it, I just found strengths where there was none. That night was remarkable because just by touching his skin, I felt how lucky I was to have the one whom I love, to feel in love. Not because I wasn't, but it was just the thought of losing the person whom you deeply love, the fear of not seeing him again. So then I just held fast more on to him.

The next morning, Jacob talked to me and told me that if it was okay, he would like to stay in school. I understood that he still would like his friends and space; he was prowling until Jacob just decided to tell me.

But how would I not understand? I certainly smiled and said, "Okay, sweetheart. It's great, but you are going to ride the bus. I know that that will be an exciting new experience, and Daddy and I will always wait for you at home. As you know, Mommy has to stay home now, but I am proud of you, and you did make a good choice."

Then Jacob left for school. After Jacob left, Patricia and I started the therapy since while I was talking with Jacob and putting him in the bus, Patricia got the time to fed Kevin.

The therapy, basically, was to enhance the sense of touch to stimulate movements. We used to give him warm baths, and then we massaged all his muscles and stretched them— neck, head, fingers, toes, and every part of his body. The process was just a person who went through a thrombosis, but my heart was pumping. Every second was a leap of faith that was seizing me. And how could it not be that way? Since that time I saw him, I inwardly felt something that I could not atone but just feel it. At the moment, I was feeling something that did not need to be explain but the steadfastness of the reliability that it attested, and it spread out in me as replete serenity. I guess being fickle was not an option from time to time.

Brian came with Emma and Rose that afternoon to visit. We were in the backyard, just taking advantage of the good weather. We were sitting for a while, just talking, sitting by the patio table. Jacob was talking about the day he performed the play, and he was all happy, telling Kevin and I how he was able to do it and how he felt after the clapping, even though his palms were sweating just a bit. He did the play for us, and Patricia was in a role too.

Jacob just kept running and playing while Patricia and I were helping Kevin to his therapy with some movements for the jaw, helping him to chew on a toothbrush and some rubber to stimulate more. It was not since he did not lose all sensation of movements, but he was responding. Every time we did it, he did it faster and constantly. Then while we laid him down, we saw Brian coming with Emma and Rose since there was a way around from the front of the house to the backyard. Jacob jumped out of excitement when he saw Rose.

We were just starting some workout for the therapy session for his legs, arms, and back so that he could gain strength and be able to move and stand, maybe not walk but with just the effort of standing—that was the goal.

Meanwhile, Emma and Brian sat beside us. Brian was all excited about new clients and the firm and how Rose wanted to come and play and that she wanted maybe to sleepover some time. Emma brought some food and some games for Jacob and Rose to play since they knew each other almost since birth.

Emma knew what Jacob enjoyed to play the most. The afternoon passed too quickly. I invited them to stay for dinner, and we all indeed had a fantastic evening. Then it was time for Kevin to rest and go to sleep since the therapy sessions were getting a little longer and intensive every time and some new exercises were added to the routine. I went out to talk a bit more with Brian and Emma, while Jacob and Rose did not want to say goodbye. My parents called me right about when I was putting Jacob to sleep. Jacob knew it was them, so he wanted to talk to them and tell them all about the day and how happy and blessed he was for everyone in his life, including them. I would say Jacob always surprised me in the least moment that I expected, and that was always a good feeling afterward.

In my quiet times, when the night could freeze my thoughts and while everyone was sleeping, my emotions would crash into one another, and the silence was the reflection that the mirror confronted me to see. As the days passed and with the therapies and mixing routines, there were times that we put Kevin inside a pool, and sometimes we put him into warm water, depending on the exercises and his muscles. He was finally starting to sit and stay still; his back was getting strong, and his legs could stay in place. That meant that he was gaining strength that he could hold in place. He was also eating better; it was not just smashed food because we had to do therapy for his jaw. To stimulate movements, we used to put a toothbrush in the back of his teeth and in the front teeth so he could chew on it, and this was part of his speech-language therapy.

When Jacob came home from school, he used to tell Kevin how his day was, and he would also make time to try to make him practice some words, teach Kevin some vocabulary, and sing songs. I remember a particular time when we were in the patio. I was reading, and Jacob was talking to him, and then Jacob was telling Kevin, "Okay, Daddy. Repeat after me. Say, 'I love you, Jacob.'"

He told him, "Let's try it again and slower. I am Mr. Jacob, and you are my student."

Meanwhile, I was just observing, but Kevin mumbled the words "I love you, Jacob." I remembered it as it was that very moment when my skin was in a shocking, thrilling emotion.

I called Patricia and told her that Kevin had mumbled a full understandable sentence. It was as if the waves were finally passive from the tide. Jacob was so happy; we could not stop smiling. So the next day, after Jacob went to school, Patricia, Kevin, and I went to see Dr. Lee, with a lot of hope and good encouragement.

While going there, I found myself praying and giving thanks to God because there was a ray of sun right in the middle of the cloudy days. For sure, faith is the assurance of things hoped for, the conviction of things not seen; and that is what holds you strong, rooted, and grounded. Most people would feel empty and hopeless, just trying to look for the empty space. But grace will find you right back when you most needed it and remind you that you are not alone and God is with you all along.

When we finally got to the hospital, we waited for a few minutes. Dr. Lee called us, and he talked to us to hear about the progress and all the information about the therapies and more. Meanwhile, he was doing a general checkup to Kevin, such as checking his vitals, reflexes, muscles, trying to make him sit and stand. The doctor said that he could find reflex in his muscles, and he started to get back his sensitivity, his mobility, and his body. He was developing the sense of touch once again.

He could sit, and he could stay in a chair, holding his own weight, meaning he did not need someone to hold. He was able to just stay as well as stand on his legs and support himself just with the help of one person because his legs were not that strong as his arms yet. But that was just the beginning of recovering his mobility. To me, this news was giving more than adrenaline or excitement; there was an emotion as if there were not enough air that you needed to keep breathing faster and deeper, with bright tearing eyes. You just started living again; it was a moment that took your breath away—from white and black to vivid colors.

The doctor said that it would take a few months more, but as everything looked, it would have positive results. After we got home, we gave a surprise to Jacob. Kevin, with help, was able to stand his body. It was a little heavy for him, but definitely, he was gaining strength. Every single day after that day, as time was passing, Kevin was getting better every day. After he gained strength inside and outside, he was just encouraged. Jacob was reading and telling him about his day every day. Furthermore, within a couple of months, Kevin was talking better as well, and he gained his total mobility about five months after that day. His total recovery was about a year; he was talking and doing a lot, expect working yet.

When he was a lot better, Patricia bid us all goodbye and left, happy and blessed to see the miracle that he was, from the fact that he survived such a catastrophic accident to the time he recovered.

The next day after Patricia left, Brian, Emma, and Rose came to the house to visit. We had an imprint memory that day because after a year from the accident, Kevin had not shared that experience from the moment of the accident to the whole process of the recovery. And that day when all of us were in the backyard, he told his side of the story, and he was calling to remembrance.

Kevin started telling his story. After he got out from the office, he saw a dark and cloudy sky, but he did not get alarmed from it because it was just dark. But right after he was driving and it became windy, the car moved with the wind and shook with the sound. All of a sudden, it started to pour, and the road started to jam, and there was nothing that he could do because he had to follow from this point of the traffic. But as time passed, the storm got worse. There was a howling wind, and the thunder was just as if it were next to him; the sound of the horns and the brakes of some cars were as if weeping with sorrow in the anguish that he was feeling; he froze at the very moment of all the commotion. There was something about the day that we could just feel it was very different—a silence, a hopeless feeling of concern, and, at the same moment, a certainty of what was happening. His whole body trembled. Something startled uneasiness; a sensation of dread was surrounding.

Nothing that you see from the window was real because there was no trustworthy or clear image, and it was worse because, even though it was raining, it was humid. This made a mirage. Even though you tried so hard to focus, it was not possible to be secured of what you could see. Moreover, not all drivers were conscious of this fact, and they so wanted to hasten. The road was shaking to each sound that you hear as if a lightning struck a tree every time. The sound and the feeling was incomparable as each sound had an echo. Each time, the noise was not diminishing but increasing.

"In a tormented moment, I saw the cars passing from somewhere, but I was just following the traffic at this point."

Everything sounded as if gnawing with the water; he was stymied to see that, that made him caveat. Out of nowhere, he heard several hits; he did not know if it was the thunder or crashing cars or falling trees. It was just too intense as if his feelings were putting into a magnifying glass where he could see and feel all the sensations and feelings—his heart rising each time, and the agony and the pain and the fear. He could feel it all the way, even in the tips of his finger, and hear it even in his head. He saw a threat, not for his life, not even because of the unsecured surrounding. Anyone would think that he was afraid of his own life and of the idea of a bunch of debris of that disaster including him in it.

The thought of losing and never seeing Jacob and me again, the possibility of not spending this life together, scared him more than anything, the most fearsome and worst feeling to him.

"All this happening was as if I were drowning in grief, ripping me to pieces. My heart became so inconsolable of this thing that was coming that I truly endeavored and grabbed any idea of optimism beyond my feelings and my circumstances of my upcoming landscaping. In a second, I tried to catch every memory and, if it was possible, prolong that time to catch even more, such as remembering that day when Jacob was born, his first cry. Then I remember how I got the news that I was going to be a father. When I opened my suitcase, there it was—a sweater that my mom knitted and gave us for our firstborn.

"One memory after another, my heart was evaporating away, freezing and melting at the same time, just immersing and trying to absorb all as if all these memories would somehow soothes the outcome, and I could not see no hope. After this quick view of my life and the most important people and moments in it, I remember bringing in my mind that day we got married, waiting in the altar and looking at you—stunning and beautiful as always.

"Then the inevitable happened. I felt and heard a tremendous impact after a shadow passed in the last surrounding and then the gnawing suspense and killing silence that came with all this. But when I woke up in the intensive care, even though I was not able to do a lot of things, it was just my thoughts and me, it was as if just after drowning—you catch your breath, and your heart releases tension.

"And from that moment, I was relieved because I just remembered the first thing I thought was 'Thank you, God, because where I did not see hope, you gave me one. Forgive me for forgetting about you, and thanks for helping me and my family go through all this.' And it was as if two hands were holding life, and it was given unto me, like flowers that contained life in it.

"In the exact moment that I opened my eyes, power and strength were given to me and extended my life again. I woke up from my sleep and the nightmarish feeling from the last time that I remembered as if my heart were frozen as well from death. Because in a moment, at least for me, I could hear my heart aloud in my head once again."

Then he told me when he saw me again, at first he did not know if it were a dream. Everything looked surreal and vague, but then when he started to talk little by little, after some time that he was unable to communicate, he realized that life was more important. Just the fact that he got the opportunity to recover his family was enough, and the rest would happen with time.

From time to time, he got frustrated, not with himself but for being unable to somehow comfort me, wanting to know what I was thinking. He yearned to move and talk, just to say everything was going to be all right, and somehow also to relieve Jacob's pain.

But he got surprised with his reaction when he saw Jacob after the accident. He got goose bumps; his eyes watered just with one regret that he was no able to hug him. With a feeling that could not be expressed at the time, his heart was living again, and adrenaline passed while he saw both as a perfect picture frame imprinted in his head and heart.

When Jacob started to talk about his day in school, without any concerns or feeling of being scared, but just hugging him and kissing him, he told Kevin how much he loves him and talked about school day as any regular day without any change or something being different or the fact that it was just him communicating to Kevin. He knew that I probably talked to him, but Kevin was expecting a reaction. Every moment was priceless to see, but not being able to talk and still be able to convey and express feelings was so valuable blessing.

In those nights when time would slowly pass, when he and I were in the bedroom and I used to talk to him, he told me that those were just the best dates. He just wanted to listen to me and look at me being drunk without alcohol and floating without being in the clouds. The same moon that was witness of his accident was now ever more radiant than life itself. It was as if the light of the night was rewarding us for enduring such pain and giving us a precious moment when two hearts could just share all their explosive feelings, feelings that are really hard to describe but when you feel them, you can surely recognize them, feelings of strength and touching all emotions and feelings of gratitude.

His heart was just reviving each memory, just being thankful and melting into the emotions to share that moments, and he knew that the rest that was to come was temporary because he had won already, because life was all he needed to do what he knew would come true. And in the quiet moments, he was praying to God and meditating about God's word. He had no reason to be mad but so much to be happy, even if the circumstances said the opposite. Kevin told me he never took anything to be insignificant, even if it seemed too little, despite the process and diligence to do it step by step.

As crazy as it might sound, it was refreshing and reviving because one reason was enough to feel that way. He was grateful for everyone; to Brian, Emma, and Rose. They were the family that made his surrounding blessed. He knew that none of us had regrets or feeling of pettiness, just immersing ourselves in a huge hope and love for what was forthcoming. He could foresee his future, and that was the only thing that was worth pursuing. His recovery was coming along just fine.

"It was as if two hands extended to me, giving me a second chance, life, hope, power, strength, and more. Fears were allayed, and the worst had passed, which was death. Now the agony frothed because now life was before my eyes. And the challenge would make it difficult, but the impossible for me had vanished, and I had confidence since I woke up from that dream as all these reinforcements came immediately.

"It came and relived the things that I had to change in that instant. It reawakened me as God was one of them. I was not worried about Giselle. I knew she was strong, and although I could not encourage her all the time of my recovery, I prayed for all. Many things revived with me that day. I had to be grateful and return to the roots of the impossible, the only one who does—that is God. And I knew this happening did not come from him. It just made me reflect and be thankful. I never blamed God. Neither did I think of this as a test. I only know that all things are for good. I reminded myself that God is always with me. I recovered even in a short time. Even when I did not talk, I prayed and knew that what I learned as a child came to my mind when I needed the word of God."

***

And we had the opportunity now to begin, and to teach this to Jacob was a miracle and privilege. And that we did. We taught your dad, your grandfather, and me.

Now that you've grown, you also know God and your children too, even your grandfather Brian. He did not have the same beliefs. He changed, and he instilled this belief to your mom Rose—the power of life in God. From that point, a lot of things changed, of course, for the better. As the time was passing, our lives were fulfilling as a family. Your parents grew up together, and they became really good friends.

Jacob and Rose were inseparable, and along the way, they became boyfriend and girlfriend. They got engaged about a year before finishing their final year in the university. Half a year after graduation, they got married. They waited four years to get pregnant, and after that, all of you, my beloved ones, came along, bringing more joy and happiness to all of us.

This night is just wonderful. We're here, all together. Right, Kevin? It is always a blessing to be with you too, Brian and Emma, and now you three—Ruth, Arely, and Isaac.

Here in this backyard, we got a lot of shared memories. Now more than ever, all of us know that certain empty space we have. When we lose ourselves at some point in our lives, that is when we need God. The best legacy is the love, truth, and power from God. When we believe with all our heart, soul, and mind; with all our strength that is our all being. There might be, from time to time, some debris; but from there, we can become more than conquerors and overcome with God on our side. Life is a journey, but with a purpose to seek God, all blessing will be added into you.

We all had a turning point where we relive, and everything makes sense, and we are the perfect piece in the puzzle. Thank you for always being there for us, and at last, everything passed. And a long time ago, I found out from my mother that all that time, she was praying for me, and she told me once that she knew that I will make it through, referring to the point that I will have enough strength. She told me that she and my father picked my name because they strongly believe in God and my name Gabrielle means a woman of God, and God is my strength.

They always trust I will find my way, and thanks to God, we all did, and now you know our story, and now it is time for you to build your own, having God by your side. You had learned the importance of life and the purpose of it. Love God with all your heart, soul, mind, and of course, strength.

Time, like effervescence, passed too quickly sometimes. Sometimes pictures were part of times, but were they better than memories? I would have to say no because they could not be torn nor fade away. These memories just crabbed unto you and held you tight; they were called love and were the only ones that lasted forever.

Times are different, no doubt. This is so obvious to an eye as well is just in front of us is verily there why people feel empty from time to time. Never forget that everything that passes in our lives is an opportunity for growth. Do not forget your true path because it is like forgetting how to breathe. Never settle with the thought of just outlive is much better to breathe and relive.